MW01172974

ATOS Level: 5.74
Lexile Level: 850+

RISE, REFLECT, RESTORE

The Rise, Reflect, Restore Series is a compilation of workbooks, journals, novels, lessons, and activities grounded in the principles and practices of the Restorative Learning Model Educational and Therapeutic Framework (RLM). The series equips readers with skills, strategies, and relevant stories to inspire personal and professional growth. Follow Rise, Relate Restore on YouTube for motivational content.

RISE, REFLECT, RESTORE

Table of Contents

Restorative Learning Model

The Rise, Reflect, Restore Series uses a restorative approach to learning. Lessons and activities empower students to reflect on, process, and learn from their experiences. The **Restorative Learning Model (RLM)** encourages students to acknowledge the impact of their actions and take the necessary steps to rebuild themselves, those impacted, and their communities for the better.
Learn more about RLM at:
www.favoracademyofexcellence.org

Restorative Learning Model Educational and Therapeutic Framework (RLM)

The Restorative Learning Model (RLM) is an educational and therapeutic framework developed by Dr. A. C. Young. Using the classroom instructional process, the RLM model strengthens student cognitive, academic, and behavioral development to maximize whole child success. Learn more about RLM at: www.favoracademyofexcellence.org.

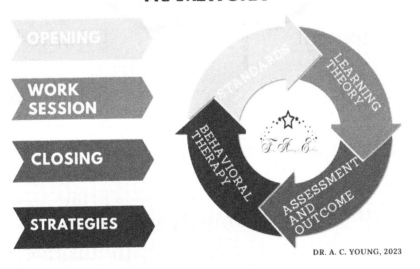

RESTORATIVE LEARNING MODEL (RLM) FRAMEWORK

OPENING

WORK SESSION

CLOSING

STRATEGIES

STANDARDS

LEARNING THEORY

BEHAVIORAL THERAPY

ASSESSMENT AND OUTCOME

DR. A. C. YOUNG, 2023

RISE, REFLECT, RESTORE

KEY VOCABULARY

Restored

Love

Appreciation

Acceptance

Depression

Habits

Mood Altering

Restoration

Judgement

Triumph

Trauma

Authenticity

Consequences

Engagement

Grattitude

Decisions

RELAX,

Unique

RELATE,

Emotions

RESTORE

Self-Esteem

Trial

Contentment

Innerwork

Inquisitive

Inclusive

MASTER OF MY FATE

The sun won't always rise and set on you
You may not experience good luck twice
You'll encounter down right brutal days
You'll meet people who aren't so nice

You may wonder if you have what it takes
When you see the success of your friends
You may even feel you have no control
Of life's strange turns and tough bends

When hard days come and emotions rage
When nights are long and days run late
Stand strong and remember this one thing
That you are the **Master of Your Fate**!

Dr. A.C. Young

Introduction

Hey Beautiful!

Do you know how amazing you are? Yes, you are perfect. We could search the entire world, and there would still only be one you. We are each born with a unique gift. Our gift connects us to our purpose in life. As you complete activities in the book, reflect on how they make you feel and take note of the activities that impact you most. If a specifc activity produces unproductive thoughts or feelings, reach out to a trusted adult to help you process and manage your emotions if needed. Feel free to keep in contact with me about your journey. I look forward to hearing all about your success!

Much Love,

Dr. A. C. Young
younga@favoracademyofexcellence.org

Zack and Tod's Stories

RLM Character Lessons

Focus Areas

Hungry Motivation

The sound coming from my stomach woke me up at 3 in da mornin. I had to get some food quick, a brotha was starvin'. I pushed the sheet back and got up as quiet as I could from the blow up mattress me and my sister was sleepin on. Didnt wanna wake her up, shoot, she just quit cryin an hour ago. I know she couldn't help it, hell, she hungry too. I gave her the last piece of sandwich I had left from lunch and made her drink two cups of water. I used the water to help fill her stomach up, cause I knew that small piece a sandwich damn sho wouldn't be enuf. I got off the mattress and looked back at my sister to make sure she was still sleep. I tiptoed to the kitchen and ran my hands across the cabinet shelves. I was hoping to find anything to eat. The cabinets was as bare now as they was two hours ago when I checked. Somethin' had to give quick. We been livin with my dad for bout a year and we aint had a home cooked meal since. Dude couldn't even keep the lights on in this raggedy shack he calls a house. Thank God for school breakfast and lunch, otherwise, me and Destiny would've been dead by now. The sad part is, they probably wouldn't even find our bodies til we missed enough days to trigger another visit from Ms. Navarro, the school social worker. Dat lady nosey self be lookin for a reason to call the state children's agency on us. When she threatened to have us taken last time, my dad started coming home every day. That only lasted for a month tho. Long enuf for Ms. Navarro to be satisfied that we were being taken care of. He was outta there as soon as she closed the case.

Now, my dad only came home when him and his girl were beefin. He left me to care for my six year old sister by myself. Problem was, I was only 15 my damn self. Wheneva I called my dad from the school to tell him we needed food, clothes or anything, he'd promise to be home that night with the items. Dude was batting 30 outta 100 with keepin his word. So I did the only thing a brotha in my situation could do, I came up on it by any means necessary. People might judge me for some of the things I did, but it's life or death for me and my sis and we ain't finna die! I need to make a plan though, we dont go back to school for two days. We gotta come up on some food til then.

How do you think Zack feels about his father? What gave you an indication of his feelings?

Have you ever had responsibilities you felt unprepared to fulfill? Explain.

Managing Responsibility

Life will often present certain tasks and responsibilities that may be difficult to complete. Our thoughts affect the way we feel and how we act. When something happens, we think about it. Those thoughts affect how we feel and what we do. The good news is, with careful planning....You can do hard things!

Task/Responsibility

Action/Process   Intended Outcome

PREPARING FOR DIFFICULT TASKS OR RESPONSIBILITIES IS A LOT EASIER WHEN YOU DEVELOP AN EXECUTION. USING THE GRID BELOW, REFLECT ON A FEW DIFFICULT TASKS YOU HAVE TO COMPLETE AND DEVELOP A PROCESS TO HELP YOU ENSURE YOU ARE SUCCESSFUL COMPLETING IT.

Task/Responsibility	Anticipated Difficulty	Plan or Process	Intended Outcome

Tod The Guard

I stood outside the grocery store parking lot in the cut. I knew that ole lady would soon come out with a cart full of groceries. She would probably be so busy talkin' on her phone that she wouldn't be checking around to see if she was in danger. Like so many of my other marks, she made the mistake of thinking she was in the "safe" part of town. She got out of the car and didn't lock her door, she was too focused on her call.

I watched her walk away and peeped the red bottom heels and the Birkin bag she was rockin'. This chick had money. If she was the type I thought she was, she was carrying at least two hundred in cash in her wallet, you know "just in case of an emergency". I needed cash and her debit card, to set up an online fund transfer account to send JT some money. JT was the leader of our crew. He moved here from California three years ago and started a smaller version of the crew he was a part of there. The crew started 8 deep but now, "The Guards" had grown to almost 150 members. I was ready to become official but still had a few things to do to show The Guards I was a true G.

Like I expected, the ole lady came out still yapping on the phone. When I heard her use her car remote to pop the trunk, I headed in her direction taking fast-paced strides. "Girl, I almost died when Sister Massey started singing her solo," the lady said to her caller. She hadn't noticed me moving toward her and struggled to hold her phone while putting her bags in her trunk.

I kept my hand in my pocket, stood close enough to her to restrict any attempt she might make to kick me, and said "Imma need you to hand me that purse". Stunned by how close I was, she didn't even put up a fight. "Here take it, just let me go," she said. I grabbed the purse, turned around, and ran off.

I knew I had about 30 minutes to check the purse for money, set up an online fund transfer account, and send JT some cash. Then I could dump her purse somewhere. It would take her about 30 minutes to call the police and lock or cancel her credit cards. I was happy the ole lady didn't make a scene. The whole thing lasted two minutes. Since the only thing showing was my eyes due to my mask, I was sure neither the lady nor the store camera got enough on me to identify anything traceable. That crazy lady actually lost time explaining to her friend what happened instead of calling the police immediately. I could hear her repeating herself as I ran away. I made it to my bike and peddled toward my neighborhood satisfied that I was one step closer to joining the guard.

What do you believe motivated Tod to rob the lady at the grocery store?

Have you ever felt pressured to do something you knew you wasn't the right thing to do? How did you resolve it?

PEER PRESSURE
RESPONSE STRATEGIES

Peer pressure involves being influenced by others to engage in an undesired behavior or activity. Developing strategies to avoid peer pressure will help you when asked to do something that makes you uncomfortable. Use the form below to build your Peer Pressure Response Strategies.

Trust Your Intuition
How do you know when something feels wrong?

Pause or Quit
List a few statements that communicate your decision to not participate.

Suggest Another Option
List alternative activites you can offer a friend when you're being pressured to do something you don't want to do.

Set Boundaries
List your boundaries below. What are some things you are committed to not doing?

Seek Support
Who do you trust to help you respond to peer pressure?

I am happy to be back in school today. I could not take another minute of my sister crying about being hungry. She wouldn't let up even though I let her eat most of the food I got from Ms. Freda over the weekend. It's like she has a bottomless pit for a stomach. At least now she'll get two full meals and a snack. I reminded her to grab two snacks off the tray when the teacher wasn't looking. I needed her to have somethin' to eat at home in case she got hungry at night. We always swiped the extra milk kids didn't want off the sharing table at lunch, to bring home. One week, we had so many, that we got sick from drinking them all night. That was too funny!

I still needed to call my dad to tell him we ain't got no food at home. I raised my hand hoping the sub would write me a pass without asking me stupid questions. When he acknowledged my hand, I told him I wasn't feelin' good and needed to go to the office. He pulled out a stack of hall passes, signed his name on one, and handed it to me without question. I could get used to him! Buddy didn't care what we did in class, as long as we left him alone. I headed toward the teachers' lounge to use the phone. I didn't want to run into our nosey, social worker today. I opened the lounge door and looked around to make sure no one was in a corner. Once I saw I was alone, I headed straight toward the phone. Of course, my dad didn't answer. I left him a message and threw in a few lies about my sister being sick and hung up. I had to say somethin' to get him to call us back. I was walkin' out when I noticed a box of pizza on the table. I ducked into the bathroom and grabbed as many paper towels as I could. I stacked the slices on top of each other and wrapped the paper towel around them. I was three seconds from hiding the pizza in my pants when a familiar voice rang out. "Put that down right now!", said Ms. Rodriguez. I don't know if I was angry that she caught me or frustrated that all hope for going to bed on a full stomach tonight, was probably doomed.

Do you think Zack was right to steal the pizza from the lounge? Why or why not?

Have you ever done something that may have been morally wrong but necessary? How would you handle it differently?

Effective Decision Making

Evaluating the Pros and Cons of a decision is an effective strategy. Reflect on a decision you recently made or one you anticipate making. Using the chart below, evaluate the pros and cons of your decision to ensure you are making the right choice.

Decision:

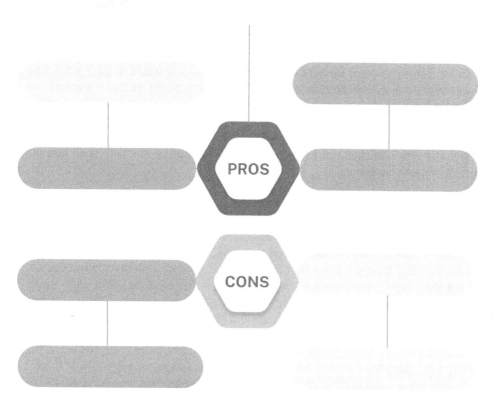

Review the pros and cons of your decision listed above. Will your decision produce more positive (pros) or negative (cons) outcomes?
If your decision produces more cons, contemplate making another decision.

How We Roll

My mama always said, "Give a person an inch, and they'll want a mile". I finally understand what she meant by that. For the past two weeks, JT added a new task to my list every day. The more money I stole for him, the more "rituals" I had to complete. It didn't matter what I had to do though, I needed to be a part of The Guards. The Guards had status and respect in our hood. Since I started hanging with them, I didn't worry about nobody running up on me. I wasn't official yet, but everyone knew JT rocked with me. That kinda juice was worth millions in our hood. As long as I can remember, I been on my own. I was what the judge called "a ward of the state". I'll never forget the judge telling the case manager to find me a foster family that would mentor me. Man, dude was trippin'! He actually believed people became foster parents because they liked kids. Every house they transferred me to had one goal and that was to collect a check off my head. Now I'm not hatin' on nobody's ability to come up but damn, it seemed like they would at least make sure I was in the house from time to time. Every time the school reported me truant, the case manager would pick me up and place me in a new foster home. I lived with a couple a whole year one time and never knew their name. All I knew was, they got high 24/7! They didn't want me there so they locked me out of the house whenever I left. One day I decided not to go back and struck out on my own, been sleepin' wherever I can, ever since.

The members of The Guard were the closest things I had to family, so I had to do whatever it took to stay connected with them. My newest ritual was a team effort. JT made me roll with Marko to steal him a ride for the weekend. I should've known the plan wasn't gonna work when Marko said we were taking a car from the country club. That fool believed those rich people at the country club wouldn't notice us. "Look ova there", Marko said. I turned around to the most beautiful Benz I ever seen. It was a big-body Benz with top-level upgrades on the inside. I knew JT would flip out when he saw it. Marko snuck up to the valet desk and mashed every Benz key alarm he saw. I looked around to make sure no one rolled up on him while he searched through the keys. He finally pointed a key toward the Benz that made the lights and sound flash after he hit the button. We ran towards the Benz ready to take off. As soon as I touched the door handle an officer yelled "Put your hands in the air and step away from the vehicle!" I assumed the position and took a deep breath. At least I knew I had a place to sleep tonight.

Do you believe JT was taking advantage of Tod? Why or Why Not?

Have you ever experienced a toxic relationship with a friend or family member? What did you do to resolve it?

IDENTIFYING TOXIC FRIENDSHIPS

Toxic Friendships are not always easy to spot immediately but over time you will notice an absence of mutual respect, trust, and support.   Use the activity below to help you identify and respond to a toxic friendship.

Identify three deal-breaking behaviors in a friendship? (Ex: A friend that pressures me.)
1.
2.
3.

How would you fix a toxic friendship?

How would end a toxic friendship?

Zack   Making Matters Worse

There was no way I was letting it go down like this. The social worker was two minutes away from calling the Children and Families Department and I knew all that only meant I would be separated from my sister. My blood began boiling inside because it felt like the social worker was fixed on making life hard for me. When she grabbed my shoulder to lead me out of the teacher's lounge, I spazzed on her. "Get your hands off me, lady!" I shouted. "If you touch me again, Imma hurt you!" I continued. Shocked by the sound of aggression in my voice, Ms. Navarro radioed for our school resource officer. Officer Parks, I need you to come to the teacher's lounge quickly!" She directed. Within three minutes, I was in handcuffs and being told to calm down. The problem was, I couldn't calm down. I was on ten at this point and did not see a reason to cooperate now. Officer Parks threatened to transport me to juvenile hall and I dared him to do what he needed to do.

Ms. Navarro was in the other room trying to reach my dad by phone. I could hear her leaving a voicemail urging him to call the school back as soon as possible. Hearing her reach out to my dad to no answer, made me angrier. I knew he wouldn't answer the phone or call the school back to check on me and that infuriated me. Officer Parks had settled me into the chair and removed the handcuffs by now so that left me free to sling papers and books across his office in rage. "Zach, you need to chill or we are about to take that ride" Officer Parks commanded. "I don't have to do nothing!" I responded. Again, Officer Parks placed me in handcuffs and led me to his police car. When I sat in his car, I realized how bad I had made the situation. Not only would I not see my sister, but she would probably still be referred to the Children and Families Department and there was no way my dad would get me out of juvie. Angry with myself for acting without thinking, I sat back, closed my eyes, and hoped my sister would be in good hands until I got released.

What do you believe Zack was feeling as Ms. Navarro grabbed his shoulder?
Do you think anyone overreacted? Who and why?

Detail an event or moment when your actions, response or behavior, worsened the outcome.

Actions *And* Consequences

Consequences are the events or outcomes that occur after a specific behavior. They can be positive or negative, depending on the action taken. Complete the chart below by listing an action or consequence.

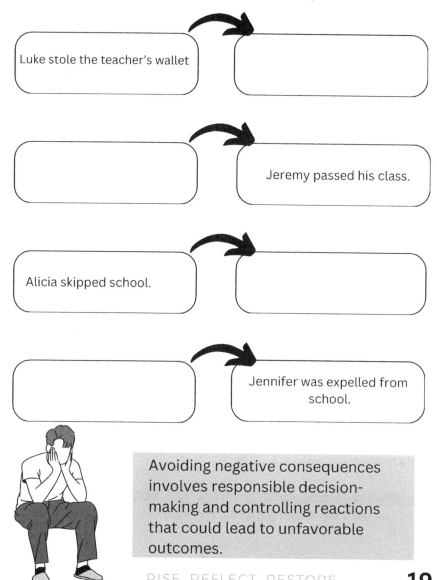

Luke stole the teacher's wallet	→	
	←	Jeremy passed his class.
Alicia skipped school.	→	
	←	Jennifer was expelled from school.

Avoiding negative consequences involves responsible decision-making and controlling reactions that could lead to unfavorable outcomes.

"You all are young, with your whole lives ahead of you. Why would you waste your life breaking into cars?" questioned the officer. We had been riding for twenty minutes to the juvenile detention center and the officer spent the entire time lecturing us. You could tell he was one of those do-gooder cops. Maybe he believed he could use his time with us to change our lives for the better. It didn't matter what was motivating him, I just wished he would shut up. I thought back to one of the conversations I had with JT about snitching. I knew no matter what they offered me, I couldn't give his name up or acknowledge "The Guard" at any time in the presence of five. We pulled into the JDC and anxiety hit my stomach. I'd been here before but my last experience wasn't good. They made me share a space with this dude named Nard. Nard was crazy for real! I mean, he was the type of dude you didn't close your eyes around. He didn't say much but his facials told everybody, he would take your life if he had to.

For the three weeks we shared living quarters, I tiptoed around the room trying not to offend him. If he went into my things, I looked on and didn't say a word. Boys from our zone whispered about his record, they claimed he would be transferred to the adult prison at some point. I heard he was guilty of everything from armed robbery to murder. Whatever he was guilty of, I wanted no part of it. I thought it was cap until lunch one day. He was sitting at a table alone when he peeped a snack he wanted on Ometreis' plate. He got up to grab it and Ometreis slapped his hand back. Before anyone could blink their eyes, Nard was kicking and stomping Ometreis all over the floor. I sat in my seat, hoping the officers would transport Nard to the adult facility for real this time. Instead, they put him on lockdown and made him visit with the psychiatrist every day. Luckily for me, my case manager had gotten me out a few days later. I wasn't sure who they would place me with this time and that fear was getting the best of me already. All I knew was because I was almost a member of the "The Guard", I would have to be ready to take out my roommate if he ran up on me.

Do you agree with Tod's decision not to tell the cop why he was breaking in the car? Why or why not?

Have you ever kept a secret when you knew telling would benefit a greater good? Why or why not?

Evaluating the Impact of Secrecy

Secrecy involves purposely keeping either positive or negative information concealed from others. Complete the activity to help you determine which secrets to keep or disclose.

LIST THREE THINGS YOU CONSIDER WHEN DECIDING TO KEEP OR DISCLOSE A SECRET:

-
-
-

PROS OF SECRET KEEPING

-
-
-
-

CONS OF SECRET KEEPING

-
-
-
-

IDENTIFY A TRUSTED ADULT TO CONSULT WITH WHEN DECIDING TO KEEP OR DISCLOSE A SECRET:

If I can't give my dad credit for anything else, I can at least say he's predictable. Officer Terry and Ms. Navarro broke a record for the most calls placed in an hour, and dude STILL didn't answer his cell. I knew he was lookin' at his phone and choosing not to answer. He had Ms. Navarro's direct number saved in his phone and he dodged ole' girl like a plague. I hoped he would at least have sense enough to ride by da crib after school to make sure Destiny was straight. The biggest downside to going to juvie was that I wasn't sure how my lil' sis would manage without me. "You musta thought you hard or something swinging at Officer Terry", the intake officer commented. He had read my charges and made it his mission to check me on behalf of Officer Terry. "I ain' swing at nobody", I mumbled. The intake officer laughed at me and continued, "We bout to see how hard you are for real in here". Everything in me wanted to swing on him, but I kept cool. I knew it wouldn't be smart to pick a fight with five on day one.

I was ordered into an empty room to take off my clothes and put on the scrubs he handed me. The name "Young Juvenile Detention Center" was printed on the upper right side of the shirt. The intake officer handed me a pair of crocks and had another officer walk me to my sleeping quarters. The room was small, cold, and smelled like a football locker room. I felt a sudden shortness of breath overtake me. The officer handed me a bed sheet and a paper-thin blanket. Then he told me dinner was at 5:00p.m. and left the room. When the officer walked off, I let the tear roll down my face. I had been holdin' it back for the past ten minutes. There was no way I was gonna let the officer see me cry. I suddenly realized I was on my own for real. I didn't know what time it was, where my sister was, where my dad was, or whether I would make it through the night. Overwhelmed, I threw the sheet and blanket across the top bunk bed and climbed on it to lie down. I knew I wouldn't be gettin' no sleep tonight so I started thinkin' bout Destiny. She would know to go to our neighbor Ms. Freda's house, once she realized I wasn't coming home. I was happy I made it a point to review a safety plan with Destiny, but I also knew Ms. Freda would call the Family and Children Services Department the moment my sister told her I didn't come home. Once she did that, there was no tellin' where my sister might land. "God, please let my dad go by the house to check on Destiny." I prayed. Hopefully, this would be the night he manned up.

Which emotion do you believe Zack felt when thinking about his sister? What indicated he was experiencing the emotion you selected?

Have you ever had someone counting on you and you were not able to help them? What was it and how did it make you feel?

Being Accountable

ACCOUNTABILITY is the act of accepting an obligation or willingness to accept responsibility or to account for one's actions. Use the examples below to describe 'accountable' actions that can be taken for each scenario.

You borrowed your mom's car and accidentally scratched the door against the garage wall. How can you take accountability?

_____

_____

_____

_____

Your friends invited you to the concert of the year, but you have a group project due in the morning. How can you be accountable?

_____

_____

_____

_____

You were responsible for cleaning the kitchen tonight but feel tired from a long and hard day. How can you show accountability?

_____

_____

_____

_____

You borrow your classmate's phone and accidentally drop it, leaving the screen broken. How can you be accountable?

_____

_____

_____

Tod   Charged and Connected

Young Juvenile Detention Center. I read that name so many times, I had memorized how each letter was written on the huge sign. I still couldn't help but stare at it as the officer drove us toward the intake entrance. When I stepped into the cramped lobby, the officer behind the partition shouted "Back again huh?" I wasn't proud that I had been here several times, but it felt good to know someone noticed me and realized I hadn't been there since my last release. I went through the motions of answering questions, changing my clothes, and waiting for the floor officer to walk me back to my quarters. "We just put your roommate in the room a few hours ago." The officer reported. I sighed realizing I was not in the mood to deal with any more crazies. I walked toward my room ready to make my new status in The Guard known to whoever was waiting. Even though I wasn't official, I knew claiming a set would keep me safe. When I entered the room, I looked up at the kid laying on the top bunk with his eyes closed. I knew immediately he wasn't a threat and this was probably his first time in juvie.

The Officer shoved me in my back and said "Welcome home", before he closed the door. The kid looked at me and said, "We ain' got no issues do we?" I was shocked by his boldness. I also caught the look of hopelessness in his eyes as he said it. I could tell fighting wasn't his go-to behavior but that he'd been through enough to risk it all if he had to. I responded, "Nah man, I'm just trying to do my time in peace". "Cool", he responded. "I'm Zack" he continued. "I'm Tod", I replied. He looked like he was on the verge of a meltdown so I continued. "What they got you for?" "Assault on a school officer and terroristic threats", he replied. I was stunned by his charges and hoped this wasn't another dude who was off in the head. "Sounds like this isn't your first time here, what they got you for this time?" he continued. "Attempted auto theft and trespassing", I replied. "I was trying to cop a Benz from the country club when five got me; almost drove off with it too" I continued. Zack erupted in laughter before he said, "Dude, you rolled up to the country club and thought you could steal a Benz?" Imagining how silly the plan was from the jump, I laughed with him. We spent the rest of the night talking about our lives and our family. I got the feeling my friendship with Zack would be life-changing.

What do you believe Tod meant when by, "I could tell fighting wasn't his go-to behavior but that he'd been through enough to risk it all if he had to"?

Has your anger or frustration over a circumstance ever led you to respond in a negative or unproductive way? What was it and did your behavior result in consequences?

Recognizing Anger

I know I am angry when....

The response I usually give when I am angry is....

A negative result of my anger was...

My reasons for avoiding negative responses when I'm angry include....

A whole week later, I was still in juvie. At least I knew Destiny was doin' good. Ms. Freda had called my dad instead of the Department of Children and Families the night I was put in here. He came and scooped my sister from the house. I was shocked when his phone finally picked up. Dad didn't want to talk to me but my sister did. When she let me know she was okay, I felt a weight lift off my shoulder. I could hear the happiness in my sister's voice when she heard my voice. Just knowin' how much she loved me, choked a brotha up sometimes. I couldn't get a good convo in with my sister without my dad shouting messages in the background. He made it clear that he had no intention of getting me out of Juvie. I laughed when he said he was making me stay here as a display of "tough love". Did he seriously think I believed that crap? He was using this opportunity to check me. He wanted to hear him beg him to help me but I would sit here for eternity before I begged for anything. It was all good though, I didn't expect him to show up no way.

The days in juvie were getting easier. I spent most of my time chattin' it up with Tod. Man, I have to admit, my life was better than I gave it credit for. Tod didn't have a house to go to every day. He lived from "pillow to post" as my mom would say. He didn't say it directly but I could tell he wished he could call someone or some place his. I peeped the way he wrote his name on everything. If he brought a bag of chips back from the cafeteria, he wrote his name on it. If someone gave him the juice they didn't drink, he wrote his name on it. Dude even wrote his name on the blanket the officer gave him when we moved in. It was weird to me. At first, it irritated me because I was the only one in the room with him. It felt like he saw me as a thief or somethin'. It wasn't til' I asked him about his mom and dad that I understood why he did it. All I could think when he told me bout them was how lucky I was.

Do you believe Zack's dad was giving him tough love? Why or why not?

Have your parent or guardian ever given you tough love? What was the circumstance that prompted their response? How did it make you feel?

Love
Characteristics

Use the organizer to list characteristics and descriptors of love.

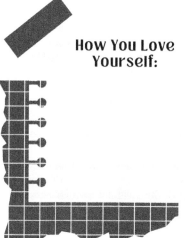

How You Love Yourself:

Words of Love:

_____
_____
_____
_____
_____
_____

How Others Show They Love You

How You Show Others Love

Zack had a way of getting me to talk about everything. He never judged me. I didn't have to act hard around him. He wasn't on that street gang stuff, he spent his days taking care of his baby sister. He talked about her like she was daughter. We were both just 15 years old, so it was crazy to me to see somebody so committed to taking care of a kid. He was less tense after he spoke to his sister. You could tell that was the only reason he was stressing about being in juvie because as soon as he talked to her, he stopped looking like he wanted to cry. One day we were kickin' it on the yard and Zack began complaining about his dad. His dad was twenty-nine years old and still in the streets. He was slinging on the other side of town and left Zack home with his sister a lot. He dropped off money when he had it and checked on them a few times a month but for the most part, he left Zack to be the parent for Destiny. Zack went on and on about how much he hated his dad and I finally cut him off by saying *"Man, quit tripping! You lucky you got a dad!"*

I must've screamed that statement louder than I realized because Tod looked at me like I offended his whole life. I didn't want him to stop kicking it with me so I decided to tell him about my parents. Zack listened on as I told him about the day my mom was killed. She had just come back from Miami dropping a package off. She had a lot of money on her that day and wanted to surprise us with gifts. She got into with some lady in the mall and was caught off guard in the parking lot by the lady and her crew. Everybody that witnessed the fight said my mama went out like a true G. She held her own for about five minutes before someone fired a bullet at her. She bled out in the middle of the mall parking lot for about two hours before anyone called for an ambulance to help her. She was DOA when the ambulance finally arrived. I was eight years old the day the case manager knocked on our door. She flashed her badge at me and asked all the kids to sit in the living room. She dialed the prison and had them put my dad on the phone. My dad cried through his words but mustered up enough strength to tell us my mom was dead. I didn't even get a chance to respond before I heard the guard telling him his time was up. The case manager didn't ask any of us how we felt, she just told us to pack our bags because we were going with her. That was the day my life changed. I knew my dad would never come get us because he was serving two life sentences in prison. The Department of Children and Families placed my brother, sister and I, in different group homes. Since they were both under five, there were more homes willing to take them. We never saw each other again.

How do you think the loss of Tod's parents have affected him? Give details to support your position?

Have you ever experienced the loss of a family member or close friend? How did it affect you?

Stages of Grief
Recognizing and Managing feelings

Initially developed as the five stages of grief by Psychiatrist Elisabeth Kubler-Ross, the model is now organized into seven stages. Listed below is a brief explanation of each stage to help you recognize various emotions in the grieving process.

Shock & Denial
The shock and denial phase of grief include :
- Depression
- Loneliness
- Anger

Pain & Guilt
The pain and guilt stage of grief are:
- Sadness
- Guilt
- Regret

Anger & Bargaining
The anger and bargaining stages of grief include:
- Rage
- Hope
- Anxiety

Depression
The depression stage of grief are:
- Loneliness
- Sadness
- Emptiness

The Upward Turn
The upward turn stage of grief include:
- Hopeful
- Happiness
- Calmness

Reconstruction
The reconstruction stage of grief include:
- Energy
- Optimism
- Peace

Acceptance & Hope
The acceptance and hope stage of grief are:
- Relief
- Hope
- Reflection

In some strange twist of fate, my dad appeared at my court case to get me out of juvie. He probably only did it because he needed me to take care of Destiny. I was just happy he ca. I was gonna miss hanging out with Tod every day, but I needed to make sure my lil sis was ok. The good thing was, since Tod and I came in on the same day, we both had our court dates on the same day. Since Tod was a ward of the state, he would be released to the case manager. Ain't no telling where the new case manager would place him to live once they let him out. I gave him my email address before I left our room so that he could hit me up when his case was over and let me know how it ended. As soon as I stepped foot in the car, my dad came at me with insults. "You gotta be real stupid to get locked up for stealing pizza!" Dad said. I don't know why I expected him to be different this time, but I did. Tod had made me see how hard life was for my dad, he even had a brotha almost appreciating him.

I wanted to go in on my dad for comin' at me like I was a lil' boy but I held my tongue. I let him get every word he had to say out and sat in the car quietly. Dad finally quit screamin in my ear long enuf to realize I wasn't matching his energy. He almost sounded shocked when he inquired "What's up with you Z?". "Ain't nothin' up with me, I just don't wanna keep going back and forth with you no more. I get it, you da father, I'm da son." I replied. Man, you could cut my dad's silence with a knife. He finally broke the silence by asking what it was like in juvie. I told him about the inner workings of juvie and Tod. Dad swapped stories with me and told me about his time in juvie and the city jail. Hearing my dad talk about his stints in and out of lockdown helped me understand him a lil' better. A few times he went missing in the past, now made sense. He let me know he was in jail. Dad came up on the bag however he could. Most times he was successful, other times he caught a misdemeanor charge. He told me how hard it was to live the right way with charges. Dad said he was workin' on being a better role model for me though. He was even gone look for a real job to help him stay outta trouble. He said he was disappointed in himself that I got locked up. He knew it was only because of my hunger that I got into the situation. He said he had a newfound respect for me because I caught a charge for him. I guess that should have concerned me, but it made me proud to know he noticed me.

Why do you believe Zack made the decision to yield to his father's authority? Do you agree with his new attitude about his father? Why or why not?

Have you ever struggled to respect the authority of a family member or trusted authority? Why or Why not?

Demonstrating Respect

Respectful behavior involves giving due regard to the feelings, wishes, rights, or traditions of others. This means even if you disagree, your posture and behavior should remain considerate. Using the scenarios below, develop a respectful response.

You walk into an office and the secretary is seated behind the desk:

A person enters a building behind you with their arms are full of items:

While dancing at your school prom, you step on someone's foot accidentally:

Your teacher unfairly accuses you of cheating, and you disagree:

A customer at your part-time job screams at you for getting their order wrong:

An authority figure speaks to you in a condescending and insulting way:

Your parent has requested you clean an area that your older sibling left in disarray:

You hear your peer make untrue statements about your best friend publicly:

An elderly person boards the city bus, and you notice there are no more available seats:

Reminder: Respect is due to everyone. Respect is the minimum requirement for any relational exchange. Commit to grounding your words and behavior in respect daily.

I had ten minutes to get to know my new case manager before we went before the judge. This was the first time I had a male voice speaking on my behalf. That mattered to me for some reason. Mr. Donald had already reviewed my file before we met. "You've had a life no child should have to experience.....I'm sorry". He said. His words caught me by surprise. He continued, "You're not a bad person son, you're just a person who has had bad things happen to them". It was the first time anyone ever talked to me like that. I had rehearsed my posture before Mr. Donald walked in and was prepared to give him a nonchalant demeanor......but his first sentence melted me like butter. He broke me down out the gate. My voice trembled as I replied, "Thanks for saying that". It was all I could say at the moment. He spent the next few minutes asking about my dreams and goals. He was different for sure. I couldn't remember the last time anyone cared to ask about my dreams. These days, I was just happy if I lived to see my next birthday. Mr. Donald asked me if I could have one thing in the world, what would it be? I don't know what made me comfortable enough to respond truthfully but I replied, "To belong to someone." Mr. Donald shook his head slowly and replied, "I see....well let's make sure that happens for you." He walked to the door and motioned me to follow him. "Let's go begin the work."

The court case moved quickly because the Judge and Mr. Donald were on the same page about my case. They agreed I needed to move to a new home, in a different community. The judge released me to Mr. Donald's care and told me he never wanted to see my face again. Mr. Donald grabbed his briefcase, looked me in the eyes, and said, "Son, you've just been given a second chance, make it count." I had no clue what he meant but something told me, I would eventually understand every word of his statement. Mr. Donald signed me out and one of the floor officers escorted us to his car. As we drove off, I looked back at the sign that read Young Detention Center. As I'd done before, I studied the lettering and silently read the words again. I planned to make it the last time I ever read those words. Mr. Donald's phone conversation interrupted my thoughts. "This is a kid I will need you to snatch back for me." I wasn't sure what he meant by his words, but I knew he was referring to me.

What do you believe Mr. Donald meant when he said, "You are not a bad person son, you're just a person whose had bad things happen to him? Do you agree? Why or Why Not?

Have traumatic circumstances in life ever triggered the way you behaved? Detail an example:

Emotional TRIGGERS

An Emotional Trigger can elicit an intense or unexpected response, forcing you to relive or reengage past trauma. Triggers often produce a behavior or response. Use the organizer below to reflect on your experiences with the emotional triggers provided and list your response

Emotional Trigger

A trusted friend or family member disappoints me in a great way:

Response

Emotional Trigger

Someone publicly embarrasses or shames me:

Response

Emotional Trigger

Someone hurts me (physically or emotionally) deeply

Response

Reflection

Review your responses to emotional triggers, how would you describe your typical response strategy?

Alternative

List some alternative responses below.

RISE, REFLECT, RESTORE

Zack   Things Were Looking Up

Things were goin' well for me and my dad since they released me from Juvie. He came home every night for three weeks straight. He was able to find a job at a restaurant near our apartment. Dad complained that it paid him pennies but at least it was honest work. Dad's new job was perfect for me and my lil' sis. Since he started working there, we didn't worry bout eatin' at night no more. Whateva the restaurant didn't sell that day was fair game for the workers. Dad said, the people on his shift always let him make food for us first before they divided up the rest. Many of them had seen us beggin' for food in the past. My dad cracked us up wheneva he talked about the craziness of working at a busy restaurant. He had to learn how to bite his tongue when people came at him sideways. I knew if my dad, a man who was known to thrown down on sight if necessary, could learn to ignore people when they tried his manhood, I could too.

When I returned to school Officer Terry added me to the circle group he led. The group was created for kids returning to school from juvenile hall. It was a required part of the reentry plan the courts put in place for kids. It was sort of like that twelve-step program people take when they are trying to kick an alcohol habit. One of the hardest things for me to get used to was talkin' in front of people. Officer Terry made us "unpack" our thoughts and feelings in the circle. Each kid pitched in and helped each other through issues as they arose. We couldn't laugh or judge nobody's story. I think that was the part of the circle group that I liked the most. All of us had a past that we were trying to recover from and we got to do it together. I kept in touch with Tod through email. He wasn't enrolled in a new school yet, but he liked his new group home. It was an all-boy's home, and Tod filled the last bed they had. The house leader was a young pastor. Tod said he was about thirty years old. He had locs, gold teeth, and understood the game better than most people his age. He treated Tod and the other three boys, like his lil' brothers. They had strict rules they had to abide by and Tod said the house leader didn't play games about the rules. Tod didn't see any of his old crew and eventually let go of his goal to join the guards. He said between me, the guys at his group home, and Pastor Chad, he was good on family. Everything finally felt right in my world.

Do you believe Zack feels the same way about his father as he did in the past? What signaled a change in Zack's impression of his dad?

Have you ever had a relationship with a friend or family member change? Was it a good or bad change? What prompted the change?

Processing Change

There's an old adage that says, the only constant is change. Change, both good and bad, is an inevitable part of life. Over the course of your life you will experience many changes such as: career change, relational change, belief system changes, etc. Learning how to appropriately define and process change will expedite your adjustment period.

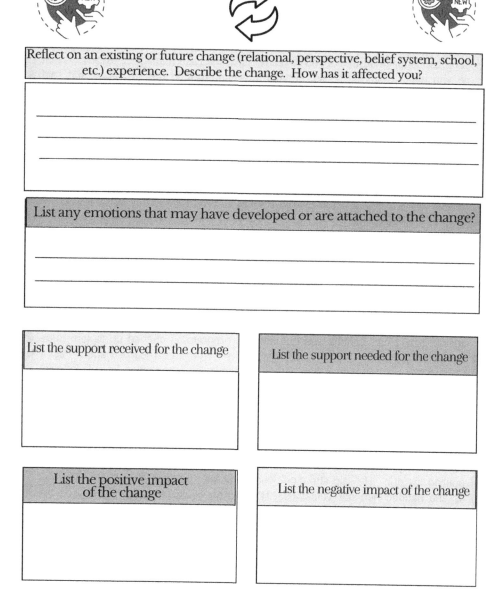

Reflect on an existing or future change (relational, perspective, belief system, school, etc.) experience. Describe the change. How has it affected you?

List any emotions that may have developed or are attached to the change?

List the support received for the change

List the support needed for the change

List the positive impact of the change

List the negative impact of the change

I couldn't get anything past Pastor Chad! I still remember standing at the door with the case manager hoping I wasn't being placed with another family that only saw me as their meal ticket. Nothing prepared me for what I saw when Pastor Chad opened the door. Dude looked like he was a King Pen. He and the case manager chatted it up for a few minutes while I waited in the living room and when they came out, they acted like a deal was made. "We'll get you enrolled in school as soon as Pastor Chad thinks you're ready." said the case manager. "Ready? What do you mean ready?" I said. Pastor Chad interrupted our exchange and said "Ready to be the man you are called to be". I gave him a confused look, let out a loud sigh, and shook my head. I could already tell he was going to be a lot to deal with. Since then, every move I made was watched, challenged, and questioned. If I came in five minutes past curfew, I had to sit through an hour-long discussion and a bible study session. I stopped breaking curfew after the first week because I was worn out by Pastor Chad's talks. I was in a new neighborhood; with a bunch of boys I didn't know and being forced to come to grips with a side of me I wasn't familiar with. The boys in the home were cool, but they weren't "the guard". If it wasn't for Zack's emails keeping me motivated, I would have snapped in the first two weeks. Pastor Chad knew how to apply pressure. According to him, he had seen it all, done it all, and been redeemed from it all. I was supposedly now a part of his "mission and commitment". He had one job (according to him)…and it was to snatch me back from "the hell I was headed towards". At least now I knew what my case manager was referring to on their phone call.

After three weeks of challenging Pastor Chad and losing every round I waged against him, I quit fighting and got with the program. I opened up to him more and actually looked forward to our daily talks. The more I learned about Pastor Chad, the more I respected him. He was deep in the game when he collided with fate. He and his crew rolled up on a lady getting money from the ATM one day. She drove a Maybach, had on $3000 shoes, and moved like she didn't have a care in the world. Pastor Chad didn't know her when he robbed her but he later found out who she was. The lady was the mother of one of the most notorious gang members in his hood. "You gone pay for every dime you taking with your life!" said the lady. Pastor Chad said he was shaken by the way she stared at him holding the gun. He said she didn't show any fear, just confidence and calmness as she handed him her valuables. He said he could tell they had chosen the wrong person to rob.

Two days after they robbed the lady, her son waged war on behalf of his mom. Pastor Chad was chilling on the block with his crew when a guy wearing a mask, rolled down the window and opened fire. Pastor Chad shot back in response but missed his target as the car wheels screeched off. It wasn't until the car bent the corner that Pastor Chad realized he was the only person standing. One of his friends had taken a shot to the neck that killed him instantly. The other friend had taken off running. Pastor Chad remembered calling his friend's mom to tell her he was dead. He said the sound of her cry pierced his soul deeply, and the guilt of that day was stronger than any prison or coffin he could have been sentenced to. He decided that night to give his life over to God. Everyone in the neighborhood knew the assassin was the son of the lady we robbed but no one snitched. The code was the code. Pastor Chad eventually moved to a new state, enrolled in a heating and air conditioning program at the community college, and joined a church. He hadn't looked back since. When Pastor Chad finished telling me his story, I realized how close it was to my life. I was overcome with emotion realizing I could have been killed at the Country Club that day and the reality of it all hit me like a ton of bricks. From that moment on, I no longer wanted to be a member of the guard. I wasn't sure what I would do with my life, but gang-banging wasn't it.

Which sentence confirms Pastor Chad's remorse about that tragic day? How did the day change him?

Have you ever experienced a moment or event that you deeply regret? What was it and how did you resolve it?

Overcoming Regret

Learning to cope with regret is an essential skill for a healthy and successful lifestyle.
Use the graphic organizer below to help you develop strategies to use at times of
disappointment or regret.

Mood/Emotion Tracker

○ ○ ○ ○ ○

VERRY SAD   VERY HAPPY

Recall the event or moment that led to reqret:

Coping Mechanism
List a physical activity you can do to help you cope: (Ex: Swimming, Reading, Listening to Music)

Implement Coping Mechanism:
List the amount of time needed to complete your activity.

Processing Regret: Use the space to detail the emotions you experience at times of disappointment or regret:

Reflection:
Now that you have named, processed, and implemented your coping mechanism, use this space to put your disappointment in perspective. How does disappointment affect your life as a whole? Are there things you can do to avoid disappointment? Reflect on those questions below:

Zack &Tod   Joy

Zack

I was in our circle group when he walked in. Officer Terry told us a new kid was joinin' us but I had no clue it would be Tod. I jumped out my chair and hugged him for two full minutes in front of the group the moment he walked in. I knew he was gettin' back in school but the thought of it being my school never entered my mind. I asked the kid beside me to switch seats so Tod could sit next to me. I knew the circle group discussion today would be on point, my boy was here!

Tod

When Pastor Chad told me the school I would be attending, I knew life had taken a turn for the better. Of all the schools in the city, I would be sharing a school with Zack. He had become the brother I never had. I decided not to tell him I was coming because I wanted to see his excitement. I knew Zack went to his circle group every Monday after first block, so I asked a kid in the hallway to point me toward the room they met in. The look on Zack's face when I opened the door was priceless! I was so interested to see how happy he would be, that I never prepared for my excitement to overtake me. Everyone probably thought we were being extra because we hugged for so long. I couldn't help it, Zack was my boy.

Zack and Tod

Seeing our excitement, Officer Terry centered our discussion topic on Joy. "Merriam-Webster defines Joy as the emotion evoked by well-being, success, or good fortune or by the prospect of possessing what one desires" Officer Terry read from his phone. "I want us to reflect on a Joyous moment or experience and share those stories today." Officer Terry continued. As each student shared their experience, the energy in the room became lighter. It was as if we all appreciated being a part of each other's moment of happiness. This was the first time everyone in the circle participated and the only time we were ever on one accord emotionally. Joy united us in ways our trauma couldn't. Even though our experiences were different, we each knew what it felt like inside. Officer Terry pointed and said, "Zack, you're up. Describe a moment or experience when you felt joy."

Zack

"Joy happened a few weeks ago for me. My dad came home with dinner from the restaurant he works at, we all ate together at the kitchen table and I told stories about Tod and I in juvie." I said. I took a breath and continued. "I felt joy because I could talk about, imagine and stare at, everything that made me happy at one time. It felt like everything was a linin' up for a change."

"Thank you for sharing, Zack. Tod, you get to share the last moment or experience of joy for us today, begin when you're ready," said Officer Terry.

Tod

"I finally have a home, a family, and a true friend I can be honest and open with, that's joy to me". I replied. I kept my statement short because I felt tears forming in my eyes. I realized this was the feeling I had been chasing since the judge named me a ward of the state. Zack stood up and gave me another hug. When we sat back down, I finally rested....in my joy.

Why do you believe Zack and Tod hugged for nearly two minutes? What do you believe Tod meant when he said: I finally rested...in my joy". Explain your thoughts:

Describe a moment, event, or experience when you felt joy. Include as many details about that experience as possible.

Defining Your Joy

Joy is a feeling most people spend their lifetime pursuing. Use the organizer below to help you center your thoughts and ideas on the concept of joy.

Three things that bring me continuous joy:

-
-
-

People that inspire me or bring me joy:

....

....

....

Accomplishing these goals will bring me joy:

-
-
-
-

Affirmation that helps me maintain inner joy:

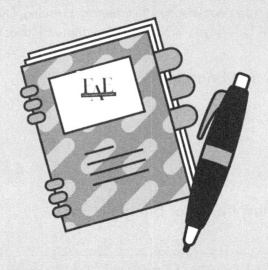

REFLECTION
ACTIVITES

The Leader in Me

Imagine interviewing for a job when the hiring manager asks you to describe your best leadership traits. Use the spaces to list your traits below.

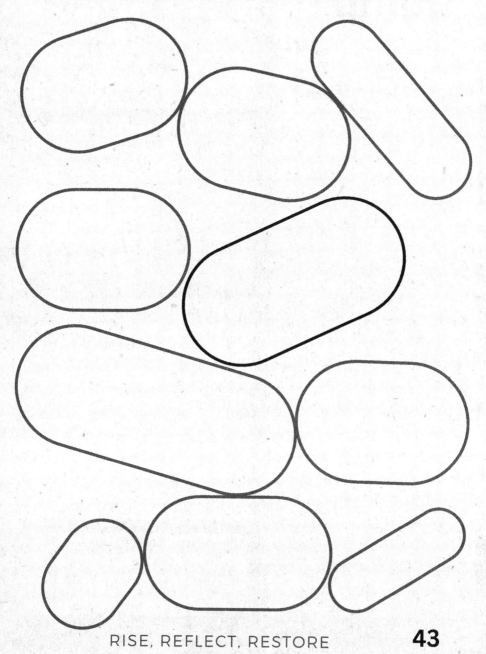

Brain Dump

Adjectives that describe me:

Things I like to do

Things I dislike doing

Topics that matter to me:

Three of my closest friends/family

Recognizing Anxiety

Anxiety is an emotion your body deploys as a self preservation strategy. It usually occurs in uncomfortable circumstances. Recognizing and appropriately responding to anxiety will lessen overwhelming feelings. Use the organizer below to help you identify and develop processes to combat anxiety.

Anxiety Triggers

- ☐ ....
- ☐ ....
- ☐ ....
- ☐ ....
- ☐ ....
- ☐ ....
- ☐ ....
- ☐ ....
- ☐ ....
- ☐ ....
- ☐ ....

Anxiety Behaviors

- ☐ ....
- ☐ ....
- ☐ ....
- ☐ ....
- ☐ ....
- ☐ ....
- ☐ ....
- ☐ ....
- ☐ ....
- ☐ ....
- ☐ ....

I know my anxiety has subsided when...

....
....
....

Three strategies I use to decrease anxiety:

....
....
....

Hopes and Dreams

List some of your hopes and dreams:

Record a detailed description of one of the hopes and/or dreams you listed above:

List your progress made toward dream(s):	List tasks you have to complete to attain dream(s):

Why do you feel it's important to have dreams? What do you believe it will it feel like once you've accomplished your dream(s)?

SETTING SMART GOALS

Goal 1:

Specific — What do I want to accomplish and why?

Measurable — How will I know when I have accomplished it?

Achievable — How can I accomplish this goal?

Relevant — Is this the right time for me to be working towards this goal?

Timebound — When do I want to accomplish this goal?

Goal 2:

Specific.

Measurable.

Achievable.

Relevant.

Timebound.

Goal 3:

Specific.

Measurable.

Achievable.

Relevant.

Timebound.

Goal 4:

Specific.

Measurable.

Achievable.

Relevant.

Timebound.

School Milestone Tracker

Use the tracker to capture key events and milestones you've experienced as you progress through each year in high school. Make a note to review your tracker at the end of every school year.

FRESHMAN YEAR

SOPHOMORE YEAR

JUNIOR YEAR

SENIOR YEAR

POST-GRADUATION ACTION PLAN

5 Minute Gratitude Journal

__ / __ / ___

S M T W TH F S

Breath before writing

Things I'm grateful for today

✱ _____
✱ _____
✱ _____
✱ _____
✱ _____

Today's feeling described in a drawing

3 best things about today

Today's Highlight

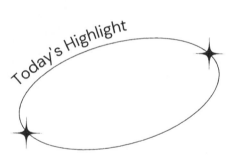

Things that I learned today

_____
_____
_____
_____

Today's Affirmation

_____
_____

RISE, REFLECT, RESTORE

Music Therapy

Jazz is a genre of music that originated in the late 19th century. The sound was developed by African Americans and became popular in cities like New Orleans. Listen to 5 minutes of jazz music. Allow yourself to hear every note. Which emotions do you believe the musicians are conveying? How do they make you feel?

Note to Self

We have all had an embarrassing experience we wish we could forget. Use the space below to write a note giving yourself advice to avoid a similar experience in the future.

Gratitude Reflection

Bad days are sure to come at various points in your life. To help you develop ways to counteract negative thoughts that might enter your mind when bad days occur, write down things you are grateful for daily below.

I'm thankful every day because:

_____

_____

Things I do to make others happy daily:

_____

_____

I look forward to this every day:

_____

_____

KEY EVENTS

Noticing moments each day is a good way to take stock of how you process your days. List one thing that happened each day (good or bad). At the end of the week, compare the number of positive and negative things you captured.

MONDAY

TUESDAY

WEDNESDAY

THURSDAY

FRIDAY

SATURDAY

SUNDAY

POSITVE THINGS

NEGATIVE THINGS

GROWTH TRACKER

USE THE T-CHART TO CAPTURE KEY CHANGES ABOUT YOURSELF OVER A FIVE YEAR PERIOD.

ME (5 YEARS AGO)	ME (CURRENTLY)

FUTURE ME

IMAGINE YOURSELF FIVE YEARS FROM NOW. LIST SOME KEY TRAITS AND ACCOMPLISHMENTS YOU EXPECT TO POSSES.

_____

_____

_____

_____

_____

_____

_____

_____

_____

_____

_____

_____

Poetry Speaks

Poetry is a form of literature
that uses rhythmic qualities
like sound and meter to evoke
a feeling, or deliver a message.
Write a short poem to describe
yourself. What would you have
the world know about you?

Who Am I?

Previously, you described yourself in a poem, in this exercise, write a speech introducing the adult you to an audience of people who admire your accomplishments.

Establishing Your Identity

In the spaces provided below, use the first letter of your name to identify positive descriptive words about yourself.

Ex: T is for Tenacious

_____ **is for** _____

_____ **is for** _____

_____ **is for** _____

_____ **is for** _____

_____ **is for** _____

Be sure to use these words to combat any description of you that does not line up to the ones you listed.

Secret Keeper

Think about your most trusted friend or family member. If you could share your biggest fear with them, what would you share?

Affirmations

It's important to recite affirmations daily to keep your mind focused on positive things. Use your technology to search for affirmations that resonate with you and incorporate them into your daily habits.

1. Ex: I am a capable, resilient, and strong/ I have unlimited potential.

Affirmation:

Affirmation:

Affirmation:

Affirmation:

Affirmation:

Affirmation:

Affirmation:

Affirmation:

Affirmation:

Habit tracker

Now that you have described who you are, let's take stock of your habits. Use the habit tracker to document how often you participate in certain activities weekly.

Ex: Watch TV	Sun	Mon	Tue	Wed	Thurs	Fri	Sat
_____	○	○	○	○	○	○	○
_____	○	○	○	○	○	○	○
_____	○	○	○	○	○	○	○
_____	○	○	○	○	○	○	○
_____	○	○	○	○	○	○	○
_____	○	○	○	○	○	○	○
_____	○	○	○	○	○	○	○
_____	○	○	○	○	○	○	○
_____	○	○	○	○	○	○	○
_____	○	○	○	○	○	○	○
_____	○	○	○	○	○	○	○
_____	○	○	○	○	○	○	○
_____	○	○	○	○	○	○	○
_____	○	○	○	○	○	○	○
_____	○	○	○	○	○	○	○
_____	○	○	○	○	○	○	○
_____	○	○	○	○	○	○	○

GOALS TRACKER

Setting short and long-term goals is a great way to ensure you are focused on your success. Use the tracker below to set goals for yourself. Be sure to include a projected date to accomplish each goal.

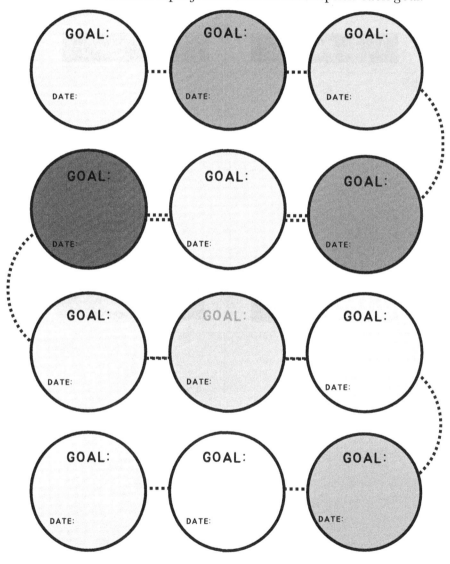

GOAL:

DATE:

GOAL:

DATE:

GOAL:

DATE:

GOAL:

DATE:

GOAL:

DATE:

GOAL:

DATE:

GOAL:

DATE:

GOAL:

DATE:

GOAL:

DATE:

GOAL:

DATE:

GOAL:

DATE:

GOAL:

DATE:

My Favorite Things

Doing what makes you happy is a valuable way to self-soothe. Use this planner to list your favorite things. Refer to them when you encounter negative situations.

My favorite people

Places I like

Favorite food(s)

Songs/Movies I Like

SCHOOL YEAR PLANNER

Effective planning is a great way to manage your stress level. Use the planner to jot down key events, projects, or plans you will likely encounter during the school year.

January	February	March
April	May	June
July	August	September
October	November	December

RLM Behavior
Management System

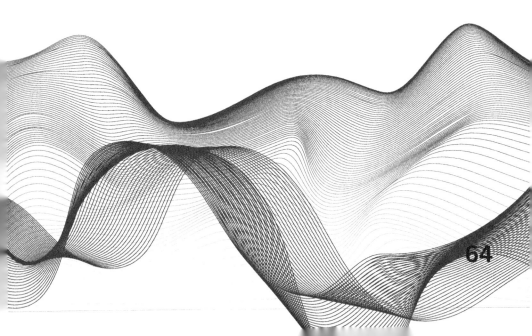

RLM Behavior Management System

Restorative practices are designed to help participants learn from unproductive emotions, behaviors, and responses that create negative outcomes or experiences. Restorative practices rely on accountability and encourage participants to repair relationships and rebuild trust. The next few activities will walk you through the stages of the RLM Behavior Management System, which include:

1. **Acknowledgement**
2. **Identification**
3. **Recapitulation**
4. **Reflection**
5. **Celebration**

ACKNOWLEDGEMENT

Acknowledgment is the act of recounting the details of an experience to help you identify patterns and triggers that create or contribute to negative outcomes.

Learning to acknowledge the emotions, behaviors, or circumstances that created your negative experience or event, requires that you first gather key details. Knowing the details of a circumstance will help you identify triggers, responses, and detrimental habits that lead to unwanted pitfalls.

The Five W method is a great way to help you organize key details of an event:

Who was involved?

What happened?

When did it happen?

Where did it happen?

Why do you believe it happened?

67

ACKNOWLEDGMENT ACTIVITY: SUMMARIZE THE EVENT

Directions: Use the details you gathered through the Five-W exercise to summarize your negative experience or event below:

IDENTIFICATION

Identification is the act of connecting someone or something to an experience or event. In this case, the something we are identifying is the emotion. Knowing when your unproductive emotions are activated, will help you better identify your triggers.

IDENTIFICATION STRATEGY: NAMING YOUR EMOTIONS

Did you know your brain processes emotions through a network of interconnected structures in the limbic system? The brain releases chemical messages that travel through our bodies to create our emotions whenever it detects a threat. Being able to identify circumstances that activate unproductive emotions, will help you avoid unwanted experiences.

Practice identifying your emotions using the below-listed strategies.

- Using a song, movie, or television show that ignites an emotion for you, jot down physical changes you notice as your body engages the emotion.

- Ask a trusted adult to help you process your emotions by describing your behavior during a certain event.

- Use descriptors. Write down every word that comes to mind when you think about a mood-altering event.

-

IDENTIFICATION ACTIVITY: DESCRIBING YOUR EMOTIONS

Directions: Now that you are armed with strategies to help you identify unproductive feelings, review the summary you developed about your negative experience and detail the moments that activated your emotions. Describe your emotion(s) in detail.

RECAPITULATION

Recapitulation is the act of <u>summarizing</u> and <u>restating</u> the main point. The main point of your negative event or experience is the outcome it produces. The outcome is the most significant part of a negative event as it reveals the impact of poor habits, behaviors, or responses. Changing your outcome will often require you to change your behavior.

IRECAPITULATION STRATEGY: SUMMARIZING THE OUTCOME

You may have learned about the concept of Cause and Effect. Cause and effect is a structure or practice used to help us understand the relationship between behaviors and outcomes. Ex: When I raised my voice at my sister (cause-behavior), she began to cry (effect-outcome). Use the organizer below to practice determining the cause and effect of your negative experience or outcome.

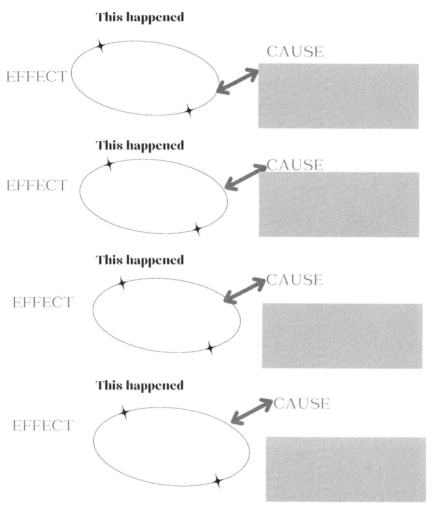

RECAPITULATION ACTIVITY: TAKING ACCOUNTABILITY

Directions: Consider the poor habits, behaviors, and responses that led to the outcome of the negative event or experience you summarized. Detail the impact of the outcome on you, those directly involved, and those indirectly impacted.

REFLECTION

Reflection requires serious thought or consideration. Taking the time to think through your negative experience or event while acknowledging the associated emotions, behaviors, and outcomes is necessary for your personal growth and development. Adequate reflection ignites positive change.

REFLECTION STRATEGY: MIND MAPPING

Use the mind map below to help you deep dive into the contributing factors of your negative experience or event. The top box is used to name your negative experience or event. The remaining boxes allow you to include impacted people, activated emotions, and poor habits or behaviors that contributed to the event.

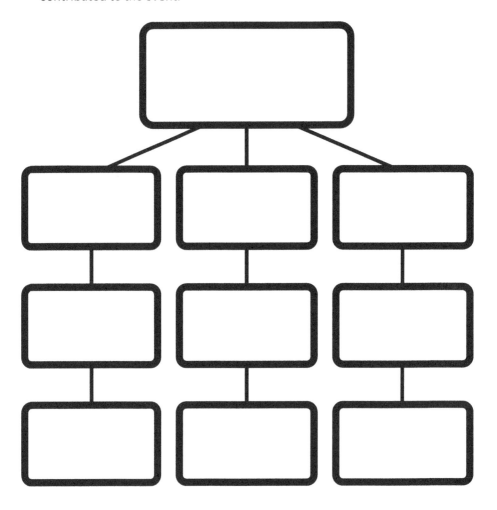

REFLECTION ACTIVITY: NAMING YOUR EMOTIONS

Directions: Set aside time to think through every part of your negative event. Develop a plan to repair negatively impacted relationships, restore trust, and build response techniques, to ensure the event never recurs.

CELEBRATION

Celebration is the act of marking an important event with a positive or joy-filled gesture. Celebrations can be used as sources of motivation, as they recognize the steps taken toward building positive norms. Taking stock of your growth and development helps to keep you on the trajectory of success.

Celebrating wins (big or small) has lasting effects. Not only does it improve your mental health and overall well-being, but it teaches you how to acknowledge your growth.

We are all just one scenario away from another unwanted emotionally charged event. The beauty is, we get to look back on all the wonderful success we had in the past, to help us overcome new obstacles as they come our way. Over time, you will notice changes to your:

Self-esteem
Motivation
Optimism
Confidence
Strategy

CELEBRATION ACTIVITY: HIGHLIGHTING POSTIVE CHANGES

Directions: Every step you take toward managing your emotions and changing negative behavior is a worthy reason to celebrate. Use the space below to brag about your successes (big or small). Each celebration serves as evidence that you are on the right track.

KEEP, SHARE, ENGAGE

Use the boxes below to help guide your next steps:

Desiring to Keep details of your restorative journey to yourself is perfectly okay. Which part of this experience do you plan to keep to yourself, list your reasons why:

Sharing your restorative journey is also your choice. If you choose to share your parts of your experience, who would you share it with, what would you share and why did you choose the person selected?

Engaging in your restorative journey requires a commitment to developing a new way of thinking or behaving for your betterment. How will you intentionally engage in your process of restoration?

MASTER YOUR FATE

82

ADDITIONAL STRATEGIES & RESOURCES

R.E.S.T

R.E.S.T. is a skill often used in Dialectical Behavior Therapy. It has been proven to help combat feelings of frustration, anxiety, and distressing behaviors. Using the R.E.S.T strategy when unproductive emotions are activated, will help to bring you back to a comfortable state of mind quickly. The more you practice R.E.S.T, the better you'll get.

R Relax. Stop, Pause. or Freeze. Take a few deep breaths before you respond.

E Evaluate. Review the facts. Observe your physical, emotional, and mental state.

S Set an intention. Employ a coping skill by engaging in a calming activity.

T Take action. Once you are confident in your ability to control your response, proceed mindfully.

VISION BOARD

A Vision Board is a creative collection of pictures, quotes, poems, songs, and anything you deem inspirational or motivational. Create a collage of characteristics that describe your current and future way of processing emotions.

CURRENT "ME"	FUTURE "ME"

PATTERNS

A pattern is a repetitive model or design. Unraveling patterns bounded by negative habits and behaviors is a significant part of your restorative journey. It will help you implement your specifically developed emotional management system. This won't be easy to do the first time you journal, but as you add entries, you'll likely notice common emotions and behaviors.

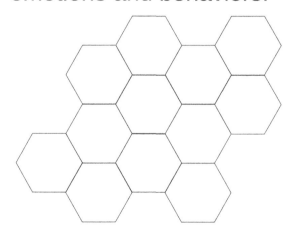

GUIDED JOURNAL PAGES

ACKNOWLEDGMENT ACTIVITY: SUMMARIZE THE EVENT

Directions: Use details you gathered through the Five-W exercise to you gather to summarize your negative experience or event below:

IDENTIFICATION ACTIVITY: DESCRIBING YOUR EMOTIONS

Directions: Now that you are armed with strategies to help you identify unproductive feelings, review the summary you developed about your negative experience and detail the moments that activated your emotions. Describe your emotion(s) in detail.

RECAPITULATION ACTIVITY: TAKING ACCOUNTABILITY

Directions: Consider the poor habits, behaviors, and responses that led to the outcome of the negative event or experience you summarized. Detail the impact of the outcome on you, those directly involved, and those indirectly impacted.

REFLECTION ACTIVITY: NAMING YOUR EMOTIONS

Directions: Set aside time to think through every part of your negative event. Develop a plan to repair negatively impacted relationships, restore trust, and build response techniques, to ensure the event never recurs.

CELEBRATION ACTIVITY: HIGHLIGHTING POSTIVE CHANGES

Directions: Every step you take toward managing your emotions and changing negative behavior is a worthy reason to celebrate. Use the space below to brag about your successes (big or small). Each celebration serves as evidence that you are on the right track.

ACKNOWLEDGMENT ACTIVITY: SUMMARIZE THE EVENT

Directions: Use details you gathered through the Five-W exercise to you gather to summarize your negative experience or event below:

_____

_____

_____

_____

_____

_____

_____

_____

_____

_____

_____

_____

_____

_____

_____

_____

_____

_____

_____

_____

_____

_____

IDENTIFICATION ACTIVITY: DESCRIBING YOUR EMOTIONS

Directions: Now that you are armed with strategies to help you identify unproductive feelings, review the summary you developed about your negative experience and detail the moments that activated your emotions. Describe your emotion(s) in detail.

RECAPITULATION ACTIVITY: TAKING ACCOUNTABILITY

Directions: Consider the poor habits, behaviors, and responses that led to the outcome of the negative event or experience you summarized. Detail the impact of the outcome on you, those directly involved, and those indirectly impacted.

REFLECTION ACTIVITY: NAMING YOUR EMOTIONS

Directions: Consider the poor habits, behaviors, and responses that led to the outcome of the negative event or experience you summarized. Detail the impact of the outcome on you, those directly involved, and those indirectly impacted.

CELEBRATION ACTIVITY: HIGHLIGHTING POSTIVE CHANGES

Directions: Set aside time to think through every part of your negative event. Develop a plan to repair negatively impacted relationships, restore trust, and build response techniques, to ensure the event never recurs.

ACKNOWLEDGMENT ACTIVITY: SUMMARIZE THE EVENT

Directions: Use details you gathered through the Five-W exercise to you gather to summarize your negative experience or event below:

IDENTIFICATION ACTIVITY: DESCRIBING YOUR EMOTIONS

Directions: Now that you are armed with strategies to help you identify unproductive feelings, review the summary you developed about your negative experience and detail the moments that activated your emotions. Describe your emotion(s) in detail.

RECAPITULATION ACTIVITY: TAKING ACCOUNTABILITY

Directions: Consider the poor habits, behaviors, and responses that led to the outcome of the negative event or experience you summarized. Detail the impact of the outcome on you, those directly involved, and those indirectly impacted.

REFLECTION ACTIVITY: NAMING YOUR EMOTIONS

Directions: Set aside time to think through every part of your negative event. Develop a plan to repair negatively impacted relationships, restore trust, and build response techniques, to ensure the event never recurs.

CELEBRATION ACTIVITY: HIGHLIGHTING POSTIVE CHANGES

Directions: Every step you take toward managing your emotions and changing negative behavior is a worthy reason to celebrate. Use the space below to brag about your successes (big or small). Each celebration serves as evidence that you are on the right track.

ACKNOWLEDGMENT ACTIVITY: SUMMARIZE THE EVENT

Directions: Use details you gathered through the Five-W exercise to you gather to summarize your negative experience or event below:

IDENTIFICATION ACTIVITY: DESCRIBING YOUR EMOTIONS

Directions: Now that you are armed with strategies to help you identify unproductive feelings, review the summary you developed about your negative experience and detail the moments that activated your emotions. Describe your emotion(s) in detail.

RECAPITULATION ACTIVITY: TAKING ACCOUNTABILITY

Directions: Consider the poor habits, behaviors, and responses that led to the outcome of the negative event or experience you summarized. Detail the impact of the outcome on you, those directly involved, and those indirectly impacted.

REFLECTION ACTIVITY: NAMING YOUR EMOTIONS

Directions: Set aside time to think through every part of your negative event. Develop a plan to repair negatively impacted relationships, restore trust, and build response techniques, to ensure the event never recurs.

CELEBRATION ACTIVITY: HIGHLIGHTING POSTIVE CHANGES

Directions: Every step you take toward managing your emotions and changing negative behavior is a worthy reason to celebrate. Use the space below to brag about your successes (big or small). Each celebration serves as evidence that you are on the right track.

ACKNOWLEDGMENT ACTIVITY: SUMMARIZE THE EVENT

Directions: Use details you gathered through the Five-W exercise to you gather to summarize your negative experience or event below:

IDENTIFICATION ACTIVITY: DESCRIBING YOUR EMOTIONS

Directions: Now that you are armed with strategies to help you identify unproductive feelings, review the summary you developed about your negative experience and detail the moments that activated your emotions. Describe your emotion(s) in detail.

RECAPITULATION ACTIVITY: TAKING ACCOUNTABILITY

Directions: Consider the poor habits, behaviors, and responses that led to the outcome of the negative event or experience you summarized. Detail the impact of the outcome on you, those directly involved, and those indirectly impacted.

REFLECTION ACTIVITY: NAMING YOUR EMOTIONS

Directions: Set aside time to think through every part of your negative event. Develop a plan to repair negatively impacted relationships, restore trust, and build response techniques, to ensure the event never recurs.

CELEBRATION ACTIVITY: HIGHLIGHTING POSTIVE CHANGES

Directions: Every step you take toward managing your emotions and changing negative behavior is a worthy reason to celebrate. Use the space below to brag about your successes (big or small). Each celebration serves as evidence that you are on the right track.

ACKNOWLEDGMENT ACTIVITY: SUMMARIZE THE EVENT

Directions: Use details you gathered through the Five-W exercise to you gather to summarize your negative experience or event below:

IDENTIFICATION ACTIVITY: DESCRIBING YOUR EMOTIONS

Directions: Now that you are armed with strategies to help you identify unproductive feelings, review the summary you developed about your negative experience and detail the moments that activated your emotions. Describe your emotion(s) in detail.

RECAPITULATION ACTIVITY: TAKING ACCOUNTABILITY

Directions: Consider the poor habits, behaviors, and responses that led to the outcome of the negative event or experience you summarized. Detail the impact of the outcome on you, those directly involved, and those indirectly impacted.

REFLECTION ACTIVITY: NAMING YOUR EMOTIONS

Directions: Set aside time to think through every part of your negative event. Develop a plan to repair negatively impacted relationships, restore trust, and build response techniques, to ensure the event never recurs.

CELEBRATION ACTIVITY: HIGHLIGHTING POSTIVE CHANGES

Directions: Every step you take toward managing your emotions and changing negative behavior is a worthy reason to celebrate. Use the space below to brag about your successes (big or small). Each celebration serves as evidence that you are on the right track.

ACKNOWLEDGMENT ACTIVITY: SUMMARIZE THE EVENT

Directions: Use details you gathered through the Five-W exercise to you gather to summarize your negative experience or event below:

IDENTIFICATION ACTIVITY: DESCRIBING YOUR EMOTIONS

Directions: Now that you are armed with strategies to help you identify unproductive feelings, review the summary you developed about your negative experience and detail the moments that activated your emotions. Describe your emotion(s) in detail.

RECAPITULATION ACTIVITY: TAKING ACCOUNTABILITY

Directions: Consider the poor habits, behaviors, and responses that led to the outcome of the negative event or experience you summarized. Detail the impact of the outcome on you, those directly involved, and those indirectly impacted.

REFLECTION ACTIVITY: NAMING YOUR EMOTIONS

Directions: Set aside time to think through every part of your negative event. Develop a plan to repair negatively impacted relationships, restore trust, and build response techniques, to ensure the event never recurs.

CELEBRATION ACTIVITY: HIGHLIGHTING POSTIVE CHANGES

Directions: Every step you take toward managing your emotions and changing negative behavior is a worthy reason to celebrate. Use the space below to brag about your successes (big or small). Each celebration serves as evidence that you are on the right track.

ACKNOWLEDGMENT ACTIVITY: SUMMARIZE THE EVENT

Directions: Use details you gathered through the Five-W exercise to you gather to summarize your negative experience or event below:

IDENTIFICATION ACTIVITY: DESCRIBING YOUR EMOTIONS

Directions: Now that you are armed with strategies to help you identify unproductive feelings, review the summary you developed about your negative experience and detail the moments that activated your emotions. Describe your emotion(s) in detail.

RECAPITULATION ACTIVITY: TAKING ACCOUNTABILITY

Directions: Consider the poor habits, behaviors, and responses that led to the outcome of the negative event or experience you summarized. Detail the impact of the outcome on you, those directly involved, and those indirectly impacted.

REFLECTION ACTIVITY: NAMING YOUR EMOTIONS

Directions: Set aside time to think through every part of your negative event. Develop a plan to repair negatively impacted relationships, restore trust, and build response techniques, to ensure the event never recurs.

CELEBRATION ACTIVITY: HIGHLIGHTING POSTIVE CHANGES

Directions: Every step you take toward managing your emotions and changing negative behavior is a worthy reason to celebrate. Use the space below to brag about your successes (big or small). Each celebration serves as evidence that you are on the right track.

ACKNOWLEDGMENT ACTIVITY: SUMMARIZE THE EVENT

Directions: Use details you gathered through the Five-W exercise to you gather to summarize your negative experience or event below:

_____

_____

_____

_____

_____

_____

_____

_____

_____

_____

_____

_____

_____

_____

_____

_____

_____

_____

IDENTIFICATION ACTIVITY: DESCRIBING YOUR EMOTIONS

Directions: Now that you are armed with strategies to help you identify unproductive feelings, review the summary you developed about your negative experience and detail the moments that activated your emotions. Describe your emotion(s) in detail.

RECAPITULATION ACTIVITY: TAKING ACCOUNTABILITY

Directions: Consider the poor habits, behaviors, and responses that led to the outcome of the negative event or experience you summarized. Detail the impact of the outcome on you, those directly involved, and those indirectly impacted.

REFLECTION ACTIVITY: NAMING YOUR EMOTIONS

Directions: Set aside time to think through every part of your negative event. Develop a plan to repair negatively impacted relationships, restore trust, and build response techniques, to ensure the event never recurs.

CELEBRATION ACTIVITY: HIGHLIGHTING POSTIVE CHANGES

Directions: Every step you take toward managing your emotions and changing negative behavior is a worthy reason to celebrate. Use the space below to brag about your successes (big or small). Each celebration serves as evidence that you are on the right track.

ACKNOWLEDGMENT ACTIVITY: SUMMARIZE THE EVENT

Directions: Use details you gathered through the Five-W exercise to you gather to summarize your negative experience or event below:

IDENTIFICATION ACTIVITY: DESCRIBING YOUR EMOTIONS

Directions: Now that you are armed with strategies to help you identify unproductive feelings, review the summary you developed about your negative experience and detail the moments that activated your emotions. Describe your emotion(s) in detail.

RECAPITULATION ACTIVITY: TAKING ACCOUNTABILITY

Directions: Consider the poor habits, behaviors, and responses that led to the outcome of the negative event or experience you summarized. Detail the impact of the outcome on you, those directly involved, and those indirectly impacted.

REFLECTION ACTIVITY: NAMING YOUR EMOTIONS

Directions: Set aside time to think through every part of your negative event. Develop a plan to repair negatively impacted relationships, restore trust, and build response techniques, to ensure the event never recurs.

CELEBRATION ACTIVITY: HIGHLIGHTING POSTIVE CHANGES

Directions: Every step you take toward managing your emotions and changing negative behavior is a worthy reason to celebrate. Use the space below to brag about your successes (big or small). Each celebration serves as evidence that you are on the right track.

ACKNOWLEDGMENT ACTIVITY: SUMMARIZE THE EVENT

Directions: Use details you gathered through the Five-W exercise to you gather to summarize your negative experience or event below:

IDENTIFICATION ACTIVITY: DESCRIBING YOUR EMOTIONS

Directions: Now that you are armed with strategies to help you identify unproductive feelings, review the summary you developed about your negative experience and detail the moments that activated your emotions. Describe your emotion(s) in detail.

RECAPITULATION ACTIVITY: TAKING ACCOUNTABILITY

Directions: Consider the poor habits, behaviors, and responses that led to the outcome of the negative event or experience you summarized. Detail the impact of the outcome on you, those directly involved, and those indirectly impacted.

REFLECTION ACTIVITY: NAMING YOUR EMOTIONS

Directions: Set aside time to think through every part of your negative event. Develop a plan to repair negatively impacted relationships, restore trust, and build response techniques, to ensure the event never recurs.

CELEBRATION ACTIVITY: HIGHLIGHTING POSTIVE CHANGES

Directions: Every step you take toward managing your emotions and changing negative behavior is a worthy reason to celebrate. Use the space below to brag about your successes (big or small). Each celebration serves as evidence that you are on the right track.

ACKNOWLEDGMENT ACTIVITY: SUMMARIZE THE EVENT

Directions: Use details you gathered through the Five-W exercise to you gather to summarize your negative experience or event below:

IDENTIFICATION ACTIVITY: DESCRIBING YOUR EMOTIONS

Directions: Now that you are armed with strategies to help you identify unproductive feelings, review the summary you developed about your negative experience and detail the moments that activated your emotions. Describe your emotion(s) in detail.

RECAPITULATION ACTIVITY: TAKING ACCOUNTABILITY

Directions: Consider the poor habits, behaviors, and responses that led to the outcome of the negative event or experience you summarized. Detail the impact of the outcome on you, those directly involved, and those indirectly impacted.

REFLECTION ACTIVITY: NAMING YOUR EMOTIONS

Directions: Set aside time to think through every part of your negative event. Develop a plan to repair negatively impacted relationships, restore trust, and build response techniques, to ensure the event never recurs.

CELEBRATION ACTIVITY: HIGHLIGHTING POSTIVE CHANGES

Directions: Every step you take toward managing your emotions and changing negative behavior is a worthy reason to celebrate. Use the space below to brag about your successes (big or small). Each celebration serves as evidence that you are on the right track.

ACKNOWLEDGMENT ACTIVITY: SUMMARIZE THE EVENT

Directions: Use details you gathered through the Five-W exercise to you gather to summarize your negative experience or event below:

IDENTIFICATION ACTIVITY: DESCRIBING YOUR EMOTIONS

Directions: Now that you are armed with strategies to help you identify unproductive feelings, review the summary you developed about your negative experience and detail the moments that activated your emotions. Describe your emotion(s) in detail.

RECAPITULATION ACTIVITY: TAKING ACCOUNTABILITY

Directions: Consider the poor habits, behaviors, and responses that led to the outcome of the negative event or experience you summarized. Detail the impact of the outcome on you, those directly involved, and those indirectly impacted.

REFLECTION ACTIVITY: NAMING YOUR EMOTIONS

Directions: Set aside time to think through every part of your negative event. Develop a plan to repair negatively impacted relationships, restore trust, and build response techniques, to ensure the event never recurs.

CELEBRATION ACTIVITY: HIGHLIGHTING POSTIVE CHANGES

Directions: Every step you take toward managing your emotions and changing negative behavior is a worthy reason to celebrate. Use the space below to brag about your successes (big or small). Each celebration serves as evidence that you are on the right track.

ACKNOWLEDGMENT ACTIVITY: SUMMARIZE THE EVENT

Directions: Use details you gathered through the Five-W exercise to you gather to summarize your negative experience or event below:

IDENTIFICATION ACTIVITY: DESCRIBING YOUR EMOTIONS

Directions: Now that you are armed with strategies to help you identify unproductive feelings, review the summary you developed about your negative experience and detail the moments that activated your emotions. Describe your emotion(s) in detail.

RECAPITULATION ACTIVITY: TAKING ACCOUNTABILITY

Directions: Consider the poor habits, behaviors, and responses that led to the outcome of the negative event or experience you summarized. Detail the impact of the outcome on you, those directly involved, and those indirectly impacted.

REFLECTION ACTIVITY: NAMING YOUR EMOTIONS

Directions: Set aside time to think through every part of your negative event. Develop a plan to repair negatively impacted relationships, restore trust, and build response techniques, to ensure the event never recurs.

CELEBRATION ACTIVITY: HIGHLIGHTING POSTIVE CHANGES

Directions: Every step you take toward managing your emotions and changing negative behavior is a worthy reason to celebrate. Use the space below to brag about your successes (big or small). Each celebration serves as evidence that you are on the right track.

ACKNOWLEDGMENT ACTIVITY: SUMMARIZE THE EVENT

Directions: Use details you gathered through the Five-W exercise to you gather to summarize your negative experience or event below:

IDENTIFICATION ACTIVITY: DESCRIBING YOUR EMOTIONS

Directions: Now that you are armed with strategies to help you identify unproductive feelings, review the summary you developed about your negative experience and detail the moments that activated your emotions. Describe your emotion(s) in detail.

RECAPITULATION ACTIVITY: TAKING ACCOUNTABILITY

Directions: Consider the poor habits, behaviors, and responses that led to the outcome of the negative event or experience you summarized. Detail the impact of the outcome on you, those directly involved, and those indirectly impacted.

REFLECTION ACTIVITY: NAMING YOUR EMOTIONS

Directions: Set aside time to think through every part of your negative event. Develop a plan to repair negatively impacted relationships, restore trust, and build response techniques, to ensure the event never recurs.

CELEBRATION ACTIVITY: HIGHLIGHTING POSITIVE CHANGES

Directions: Every step you take toward managing your emotions and changing negative behavior is a worthy reason to celebrate. Use the space below to brag about your successes (big or small). Each celebration serves as evidence that you are on the right track.

ACKNOWLEDGMENT ACTIVITY: SUMMARIZE THE EVENT

Directions: Use details you gathered through the Five-W exercise to you gather to summarize your negative experience or event below:

IDENTIFICATION ACTIVITY: DESCRIBING YOUR EMOTIONS

Directions: Now that you are armed with strategies to help you identify unproductive feelings, review the summary you developed about your negative experience and detail the moments that activated your emotions. Describe your emotion(s) in detail.

RECAPITULATION ACTIVITY: TAKING ACCOUNTABILITY

Directions: Consider the poor habits, behaviors, and responses that led to the outcome of the negative event or experience you summarized. Detail the impact of the outcome on you, those directly involved, and those indirectly impacted.

REFLECTION ACTIVITY: NAMING YOUR EMOTIONS

Directions: Set aside time to think through every part of your negative event. Develop a plan to repair negatively impacted relationships, restore trust, and build response techniques, to ensure the event never recurs.

CELEBRATION ACTIVITY: HIGHLIGHTING POSTIVE CHANGES

Directions: Every step you take toward managing your emotions and changing negative behavior is a worthy reason to celebrate. Use the space below to brag about your successes (big or small). Each celebration serves as evidence that you are on the right track.

About the Author:

DR. A. C. YOUNG IS A VETERAN EDUCATOR, WHO HAS COMMITTED HER LIFE'S WORK TO ESTABLISHING EDUCATIONAL AND SOCIAL DEVELOPMENT PROGRAMS FOR STUDENTS. SHE HAS SERVED IN VARIOUS ROLES IN EDUCATION FROM TEACHER, PRINCIPAL AND NOW EXECUTIVE DIRECTOR. SHE APPRECIATES OPPORTUNITIES TO HELP LEADERS TRANSFORM THEIR HABITS FOR THE BETTERMENT OF THEMSELVES AND THE PEOPLE THEY SERVE.

Always remember to:

RISE
REFLECT
and RESTORE

You got this!

Made in the USA
Middletown, DE
09 September 2024

60669284R00097